DATE DUE			

THE TECHNOLOGY OF ANCIENT CHINA

Robert Greenberger

rosen
central™

The Rosen Publishing Group, Inc., New York

Published in 2006 by The Rosen Publishing Group, Inc.
29 East 21st Street, New York, NY 10010

First Edition

Library of Congress Cataloging-in-Publication Data

Greenberger, Robert.
The technology of ancient China/Robert Greenberger.
    p. cm.—(The technology of the ancient world)
Includes bibliographical references and index.
ISBN 1-4042-0558-6 (library binding)
1. Technology—China—History—Juvenile literature. 2. China—Civilization—To 221 B.C.—Juvenile literature. 3. China—Civilization—221 BC–960 AD—Juvenile literature. I. Title. II. Series.
T27.C5G74 2005
609.51—dc22

                                                                                    2005011815

Manufactured in the United States of America

On the cover: A painting from the seventeenth century AD shows scribes copying *Tao te King* (The Book of the Way and Its Virtue), which, according to legend, was written by Lao Zi (Lao Tzu) around 600 BC. Inset: This bronze reconstruction of a seismograph is based on Zhang Heng's seismograph, which he invented in AD 132.

CONTENTS

LEARNING ABOUT THE LAND

As humans settled around the world, they found ways to survive heat and cold and to trap and prepare food—the vital skills that allowed them to endure and even thrive during the Stone Age, beginning more than 2 million years ago. Clusters of humans created unique survival methods depending on the materials at hand locally. Using the available resources allows people to progressively invent new tools and practices to meet their needs. This process is commonly known as technology. In this book, readers will learn about Chinese technology from the end of the Stone Age, which many historians date to around 6000 BC for China, to the end of the Qin dynasty, around 207 BC.

Nomadic tribes began to settle near the great rivers of Asia around 6000 BC. The rivers provided fish for nourishment and water to grow edible plants. Small communities resulted, from which the Chinese people have prospered. Unlike many other people, the Chinese sought to find a balance between preserving the land and using it.

Other features of the land isolated the Chinese. Mountains and deserts in the northeastern portion of the Asian continent were obstacles to travel. Because of their remote location, the Chinese flourished mostly independent of foreigners. Outside influences would not be felt for many centuries, after the Chinese had established their own ways of life.

In this painting on silk from the seventeenth century, Emperor Mu Wang (about 985–907 BC) of the Zhou dynasty is pictured riding in his chariot. The ancient Chinese invented or improved many technologies involving land transportation, including the horse harness, saddle, stirrup, bit, and chariot axle.

AGRICULTURE AND FOOD PRODUCTION

The nomadic tribes that wandered around what is now known as China lived off the land, eating whatever grew naturally or could be hunted or fished. These people settled in this portion of Asia about 50,000 years ago and were hunters and gatherers.

Wild rice grew along the Yangtze River. Early evidence shows that, in the south, the Chinese cultivated rice from seeds they had put aside as early as about 7000 BC. They began using tools with wooden handles and blades made from animal bones to turn the soil and plant rice by hand. Because they lacked plentiful animal manure for fertilizer, they used human waste, which enriched the soil so that they could reuse the land year after year.

The people of the Yangshao culture lived during the Neolithic period some 5,000 to 7,000 years ago. They are named after Yangshao

Village, which was discovered in Henan province by an archaeologist in 1921. The Yangshao chose to settle along the banks of the Yellow River—or *Huang He*—which is named for the rich, yellow earth known as loess. Today this area is considered the cradle of Chinese civilization, with the Yangshao having settled there around 5000 BC.

The fertile soil enabled the Yangshao to grow millet, barley, and wheat. Around 4000 BC, they raised pigs, sheep, oxen, and dogs, and they built wooden homes covered with mud and roofs of thatched reeds. The Yangshao used strips of clay to make red or gray pottery, which they usually painted with geometric designs and fired in kilns at temperatures around 1,652° Fahrenheit (900° Celsius). They used the pottery for storage and burial purposes. The Yangshao civilization peaked around 3000 BC, as settlements expanded toward the west, and ended as a culture sometime around 1500 BC.

The Longshan culture developed around 3000 BC, south and east of the Yangshao. These people, who are named after a town archaeologists discovered in Shandong province, were more advanced than the Yangshao.

They built villages around Hangzhou Bay, at the mouth of the mighty Yangtze River (or *Chang Tiang*). The marshy land was good for growing rice as well as millet. The people also raised cattle and sheep and baked bricks for the construction of sturdy homes. They developed the notion of walled communities along the edges of rivers, providing the inhabitants with protection from nomadic tribes. Given their increasing sophistication, the Longshan grew stronger than the Yangshao, and spread farther east. The Longshan as a distinct civilization lasted until about the mid-second millennium BC.

Early Farming

The Chinese have been credited with being among the first people on Earth to grow oranges, peaches, sugarcane, and tea. The earliest animals they bred were sheep and chickens, starting around 4000 BC. In addition to cultivating rice, the people were able to domesticate pigs and cattle in larger numbers because they had pens in which to keep them. Wheat was grown in abundance and, by 3000 BC, an early form of what we know as pasta had been created.

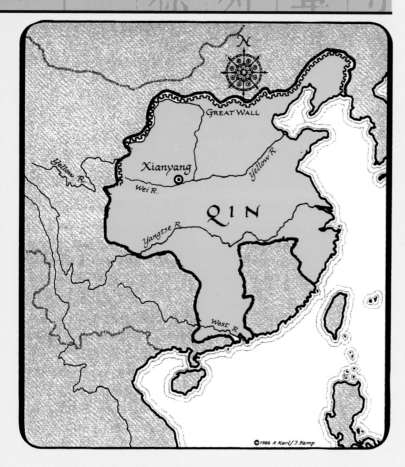

This map shows the area of Asia that was ruled by the Qin dynasty, from 221 to about 207 BC. China, or the People's Republic of China, as the country is known today, got its name from the Qin (Ch'in) Empire. The Great Wall, the building of which began under the first Qin emperor, is indicated on the map.

Between 5000 and 3000 BC, the Longshan also made pottery, although around 3000 BC they used a potter's wheel to fashion their ceramics. Unlike the Yangshao red or gray pots, the Longshan pottery was black and unpainted. These products provided both cultures with smaller, portable storage units for food.

Working the Land

As the communities became organized, the Chinese invented a way to record their history. They wrote on animal bones, which has provided archaeologists with valuable information about what might have occurred in the distant past. Not much is known about the Xia dynasty, which is mentioned in legends and traditionally dated from 2205 to 1806 BC. The Xia dynasty is considered to be the first dynasty, but many historians believed that it was mythic because no examples of its writings have been found. Starting in 1959,

THE ANCIENT CHINESE DYNASTIES

A dynasty is a series of rulers from the same family. Chinese government followed this system until the early twentieth century. The following dynasty names and periods of rule are covered in this book.

Dates	Dynasty
2205–1806 BC	Xia
1600–1300 BC	Shang (prophase, an early period marked by expansion of land holdings under the rulers)
1300–1046 BC	Shang (anaphase, a later period marked by consolidation of power and improvements in lifestyle)
1046–771 BC	Western Zhou
770–256 BC	Eastern Zhou (With the royal line being broken, the Eastern Zhou dynasty was divided into two subperiods: the Spring and Autumn and the Warring States periods.)
770–476 BC	Spring and Autumn period
475 BC –221 BC	Warring States period
221–207 BC	Qin
206 BC–AD 24	Western Han
25–220	Eastern Han
220	China is divided into the Wu, Shu, and Wei kingdoms (Three Kingdoms period)

excavations at Erlitous, in Henan province, uncovered what was most likely a capital of the Xia dynasty, proving the ancient beliefs true. The site showed that the people were direct ancestors of the Longshan and were predecessors of the people known as the Shang. As villages expanded, so too did leadership, with rulers flourishing to become regional kings. The kings then passed their titles and power down to male heirs, in lines of succession known as dynasties.

According to legend, Yu, known as the Great Engineer and the first king of the Xia dynasty, dug channels in the Yellow River. These channels prevented the river from its frequent flooding and allowed farmers to improve irrigation of their crops. The legend maintains that Yu worked thirteen years without stopping and that his channels stretched nearly 700 miles (1,127 kilometers) in length. In the years following Yu, the people also learned how to build dikes, or artificial watercourses, to better control the water for their needs.

Once settled, people had the chance to explore their homeland. As they learned about their visible world, they also dug deep and saw what lay under the surface. For example, the Chinese developed a stone drill and then dug deep wells to tap into underground salty water called brine. They brought the water to the surface by using bamboo tubes. Once the brine dried in the sun, they could extract the salt crystals, which would then be used as a meat preservative.

The Chinese also found that terracing the land turned a sloping hill into

Quern stones, such as these pictured here, were used in China at least 10,000 years ago to grind wheat into flour. Producing flour by rubbing wheat by hand took several hours. The Chinese used querns and mortars and pestles for milling and grinding rice and millet.

This carving on a brick from about 206 BC to AD 220 shows a farmer using an ox-drawn plow. The Chinese made the world's first iron plows. Their iron casting techniques enabled them to invent the moldboard, the part that turns the soil without clogging the plowshare.

a series of levels. The terraces allowed farmers to increase the amount of rice they grew in a previously unwieldy area. The people did most of their farming by hand, first using wooden plows and then, by the sixth century BC, iron plows. They harvested with a sickle. People still worked with their hands, husking rice and beating grain against a slatted frame to thresh it.

Working with Metal

As the Chinese learned to forge iron from raw materials using furnaces similar to those used for baking pottery, they created new tools. These tools included plows that helped them to use the land more efficiently for planting. Iron also enabled them to invent tools for the improved milling of grain.

The earliest iron plow found dates from about the 500s BC. It was a flat V-shaped piece, mounted on wooden poles and handles. By the third century BC, when iron tools were made using improved casting methods, the plowshare called the *kuan* (the moldboard plow) came into use and rapidly spread over the next two centuries. The kuan had a central piece that ended in a sharp point for digging the soil. It also had wings that slanted up toward the

This illustration of a wheelbarrow appeared in *Tian Gong Kai Wu* (Exploitation of the Works of Nature), a book about traditional science and technology in China. Written by Song Yingxing in 1637, the book includes descriptions and illustrations of various Chinese inventions and processes in agriculture, handicrafts, and transportation. The Chinese invented the wheelbarrow sometime in the first century BC.

center to fling the soil off the plow and lessen friction. These human-sized plows grew more sophisticated in form over the years, with the design cutting down on friction as the earth was carved and moved aside.

With the new plows came the advent of contour plowing. However, farmers recognized that the iron was too heavy to pull and was injuring the horses and oxen. Around the fourth century BC, blacksmiths fashioned a harness for horses that wrapped around the chest instead of the neck. This development, called the trace harness, enabled the animals to pull heavy loads, such as harvested grains or vegetables. Between the fourth and first centuries BC, the collar harness was used on horses for pulling transportation-related vehicles, such as war chariots.

Water buffalo–drawn carts were created to plant seeds in the furrows. Complicated harrows were used to pulverize and smooth the soil in finer seedbeds. Mills used waterpower to make grinding flour easier. By the late second century BC, the multitube seed drill, made of iron, was invented, allowing regulated and faster planting in straight rows and becoming the model for farmers around the world.

Although it may have existed earlier, around the first century AD, the Chinese invented the square-pallet chain pump, which became an invaluable aid to farmers. A chain moved between square pallets that carried excavated soil or water from lower to higher levels. The average single-pump device carried water 15 feet (4.6 meters) up, which contributed to the improvement of terraced rice farming.

Beyond Eating

Plants and trees had other uses besides food. For example, the lacquer tree's sap, after the elimination of certain impurities and excess water, was found to provide sheen for crafts. Over time, the Chinese developed lacquer production and used lacquer for decoration in furniture, chariots, utensils, and other objects. The process involved hundreds of layers of the thin lacquer fluid to achieve the finished look. Once the lacquer dried, artisans carved designs on the polished surfaces of chairs, wall screens, tables, and vases.

The Chinese also invented new tools to help them transport materials from the fields to their villages. One invention was the wheelbarrow, made in the first century BC. This simple tool, nicknamed the wooden ox and the gliding horse, dramatically improved the lot of farmers by enabling them to move heavy loads. By 118 AD, wheelbarrows were plentiful and were documented in Chinese illustrations. The wheelbarrow called the wooden ox was believed to be pulled using handles in front of a wooden frame and a wheel, whereas the one called the gliding horse was thought to be pushed by using handles that were behind the frame and wheel. Similarly, the yoke, a long pole that could be carried behind a person's neck and across the shoulders, enabled people to carry water, grain, or other items with less physical strain.

COMMUNICATION

It was sometime during the legendary Xia dynasty in the third millennium BC that the Chinese people first began to write. The people used symbols known as pictographs to represent words and objects. At first, these pictographs were written on large animal bones such as cattle shoulder blades and the underside of tortoise shells. The pictographs evolved over time and a complete written language developed around 1000 BC. Archaeologists first discovered this writing in 1899, when they found ancient bits of shell with markings on them near the city of Beijing. Through the years, a large number of these were collected, and research showed that they were the antecedents to the current written language of China. Early on, the number of pictographs totaled 80,000. Today only a few thousand are regularly used.

Oracle Bones

The writings on bones and shells were part of a method of prophecy known as scapulimancy. A diviner or fortune-teller wrote a question on the shell or polished bone, known as an oracle bone. The diviner next applied heated metal to the underside of the bone. When cracks became visible, the diviner then interpreted the answer to the question based on how the bone cracked.

Pictographs have also been found on pottery and bronze. The Chinese began making bronze—a mixture of copper and tin to which they also added lead objects—around the eighteenth century BC. By the time of the Bronze Age (1800–771 BC), sophisticated calligraphy reflected a great respect for the written word as well as the artistry of the writer.

This oracle bone with writing dates from the fourteenth to thirteenth centuries BC. Oracle bones contain the earliest examples of Chinese scripts and where usually written on tortoise shells or the scapulae (shoulder blades) of oxen.

Unification

In 221 BC, China was unified under a king of the Qin state, Ying Zheng, who first ruled as king of Qin in 247 BC and who took the name Qin Shi (which means "first" or "primary" of the Qin state) Huangdi (which means "August emperor"). He was the first king denoted as emperor across the land. Qin Shi Huangdi's unified rule lasted eleven years, but in that time he did much to establish China as a growing country. Qin Shi Huangdi and his grand councillor Li Si issued a series of decrees that forever changed

秦始皇

Qin Shi Huangdi, pictured here in a painting from the AD 1700s, created the first unified Chinese empire in 221 BC. He and his grand councillor established a central administration, constructed a series of roads and canals, began building the Great Wall, and set up the capital at Xianyang.

the country and its people, unifying them for the first time under a centralized government. The smaller states and kingdoms were now part of a nation named China, after the Qin (or Ch'in) dynasty.

Among these many laws was one that standardized written and spoken language. Another law systematized weights and measures. The entire body of new rules and regulations issued by the government of China created a bureaucracy that maintained law and order.

During the Qin dynasty (221–207 BC), Qin Shi Huangdi's orders and records were kept on slips of wood or bamboo. Scientific works and artistic works such as poetry were written instead on silk. These writings on silk were known as *boshu*.

Papermaking

Sima Qian, a historian and astrologer of the Western Han dynasty, wrote the first history of the country. (It should be noted that in China, the individual's surname, or family name, is written first, and his or her given name comes second.) He compiled this historic work on bamboo strips in 100 BC, before the use of paper was widespread, and entitled it *Shiji* (Historical Records). The Western Han dynasty, marked by the location of the capital at Chang'an (present-day Xi'an), was another period of explosive growth and change. It was during those years that the Chinese improved the making of paper, which had been employed by the 100s BC, although not for writing purposes until the first century AD.

Looking for a less cumbersome way to store information than on bamboo, around AD 105, Cai Lun mixed mulberry bark, hemp, rags, and fishnets into a damp, pulpy substance. A bamboo grid was fashioned and then dipped into the wet mess, covering it with a thin film. The drying substance, paper, was peeled off and hung to dry. Since then, papermaking methods have improved, but the essential idea came from China. Arabs brought the process west in AD 700 and eventually to Europe a century later.

It was during the Eastern Han dynasty that written works were housed in the country's first library in the capital. The idea of storing writings in private collections had existed since 550 BC. Libraries as we know them today weren't built in China until the nineteenth century AD. The first Chinese dictionary, the *Shuowen*, was compiled in AD 121 by Xu Shen, further standardizing the pictographs and their meanings.

After paper was accepted as a writing material by the noble classes (the people who owned the land and helped run the government), they used it to write letters to friends. Showing off their artistry and intellect,

This illustration from Song Yingxing's *Exploitation of the Works of Nature* (1637) shows craftspeople hanging sheets of paper to dry. The Chinese invented paper by the second century BC. They used paper for clothing, lacquerware, and military armor. They even applied it as wallpaper.

these nobles folded their letters into intricate designs, thereby inventing the art of origami. Although today it is considered a Japanese tradition, origami was adopted by the Japanese when paper was introduced there in the sixth century AD.

Ink Sticks

The use of ink improved writing and helped artistic expression to flourish. Writing was originally done by making marks with wooden or stone tools on wet clay. The earliest forms of ink were made from pine soot and lamp oil, which was mixed with the gelatin that was formed from donkey skin and musk. The ink was first used on stone surfaces. The earliest evidence of Chinese ink dates to some 6,000 years ago during the Stone Age. Artifacts recovered in the Jiangsu and Hubei provinces lead scientists to believe that the ink was made in a furnace where pottery jars were inverted over the fire to trap the heat. The soot was collected inside the jars and then removed with feather brushes. To form an ink stick, the soot was mixed for a time with glue, which was made from animal horns or hide. Glue made from the horns of young deer was considered the purest.

A writer or painter would wet the ink stick with water while striking it against a stone. The water would release enough ink from the stick to form a painting or calligraphy. Over time, this ink stick idea led to the writing brush.

Time and experimentation allowed the Chinese to create a unique language, both verbal and written. Their pictographs were later adopted by the Japanese and the Koreans, who contributed a similar but distinctive look to Asian writing.

CALCULATIONS

The Chinese respected the land, the sun, and the night sky and wanted to learn more about them. In early times, they believed the stars had power over humans and nature, so studying the night sky was a chief occupation in the various royal courts over the centuries.

The Chinese Calendar

The first study of the stars began almost at the time tribes settled along the rivers. Over the centuries, as people had time to study the skies, they based their computations on the location of the polestar and the way constellations (and groups of stars such as the Big Dipper) moved around the polestar. Chinese astronomers around the second century BC were able to observe what they called the year star. Its orbit took twelve years to complete. This

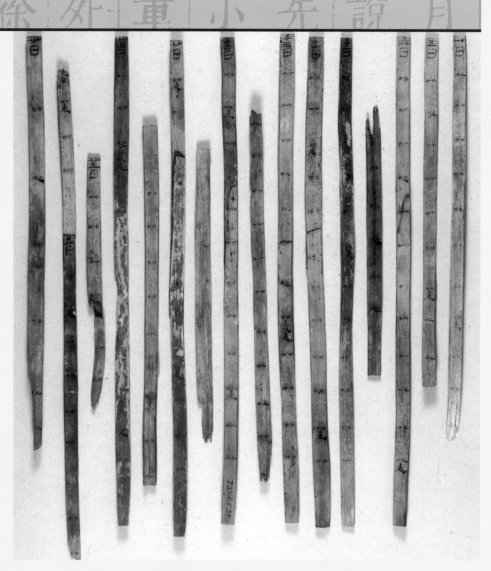

This Chinese calendar from about 63 BC was written on sixteen wood slips. The slips were to be read from right to left, and each began with a day—day one, day two, and so on.

star was later identified as the planet Jupiter.

The scientists' calculations enabled them to devise the Chinese calendar by measuring the Big Dipper's handle, which pointed north in the winter and south in the summer. From there, they figured out twelve months for a year, which was 366 days long. By 400 BC, they refined their measurements to the present-day Chinese calendar, which has 365.25 days.

The complex calculations also took into account the moon's phases, which allowed them to refine their calendar. A belief developed that

New Year's Day, the winter solstice, was the most important day of the year, signifying that the cycle of life was beginning again. The winter solstice was calculated from observations of the summer solstice, made with a special stone pillar. The shadow of the pillar was measured to find the solstices. The summer solstice was determined at the time of the shadow's shortest measure. From there, the time of the winter solstice and New Year's could be calculated.

In 104 BC, astronomers developed the calendar still in use today. The complicated measurements began with the length of the stone pillar's shadow as affected by the sun's movement across the sky. They quantified the changing seasons into twenty-four intervals that were roughly fifteen days long. The length of a year was then decided by scientists to be 365.25 days. The lunar month was said to have 29.5 days, measured from the new moon on day 1, the first quarter moon on day 7, the full moon on day 15, and the last quarter on day 21, with the month ending on day 29 or day 30. To the Chinese, the moon's cycle became the measure of choice, and they settled on 235 lunar cycles, or 19 years, as a

measure of time. To account for the remaining fraction of a day, the scientists developed a plan that created a leap month whenever there was a month when a standard lunar month failed to span two of the lunar intervals.

The astronomer Xi measures the summer solstice with a gnomon in this illustration from an edition of the *Book of Documents*, which was compiled between 481 and 221 BC. A gnomon is a shaft that is placed perpendicular to the horizon and is use to tell the hour of the day by the position or length of its shadow.

THE CHINESE ZODIAC

Each year is represented by an animal, repeating every twelve years, following the Chinese preference for cycles and ritual. According to legend, the gods asked the twelve animals to race across the river to determine the order of the zodiac. As the animals raced across the water, the ox didn't notice the rat climb atop him, which allowed the rat to leap ahead to finish first. The pig, the laziest of the animals, came in last. Certain characteristics were given to each animal; consequently, when someone was born in a particular year, he or she was said to possess that animal's attributes.

They occur in the following order:

zi (rat) Charming, hardworking, thrifty, gossipy.

chou (ox) Patient, speaks little, stubborn.

yin (tiger) Sensitive, deep-thinking, short-tempered.

mao (rabbit) Articulate, talented, ambitious, conservative.

chen (dragon) Healthy, energetic, excitable, stubborn.

si (snake) Deep-thinking, thrifty, vain, selfish.

wu (horse) Cheerful, perceptive, good with their hands, impatient.

wei (sheep) Artistic, shy, pessimistic.

shen (monkey) Clever, skillful, inventive, strong-willed.

you (rooster) Deep-thinking, eccentric, outspoken.

xu (dog) Loyal, honest, selfish.

hai (pig) Mentally strong, honest, quick-tempered.

Following the nineteen-year cycle, there are seven leap months built in to the calculations. For example, the most recent leap months were both in 2004.

Each year is represented by a corresponding animal because the beliefs of the day involved both astronomy and astrology. This Zhang cycle (known as the Metonic cycle to the Greeks) was not perfect; it was incorrect by one day every 220 years. The Chinese counted the years based on the term of an emperor, who would declare *gaiyuan* (changing the first), marking a new era. Consequently, when Qin Shi Huangdi assumed the throne in 221 BC, his third year of rule would have been marked the third year of Jianyuan (establishing the first). This practice was finally abolished during the Revolution of 1911, in which Sun Yat-Sen (Sun Yixian) and his followers overthrew the monarchical system in China.

On the Chinese calendar, a great year encompasses twelve years, a cycle equals five great years (sixty years), and an epoch is sixty cycles (60 x 60 years = 3,600 years). As calculated by the Chinese, we are currently living during the second epoch.

The most recent cycle began on February 2, 1984, and is known as *yin*, with specific years and days being assigned suffixes. In China, New Year's Day 2005 is known as *Yiyou*, in the year 4702, or the year of the rooster. The same day on the Western calendar is February 9, 2005.

Many people think the first use of magnetic compasses was for navigation. When the Chinese first used the lodestone to point to the north or to the south, around 400 BC, they were determining the ideal positions for structures like houses and burial grounds. This practice is best known today as feng shui (which means "wind and water"). The purpose of feng shui is to live in harmony and prosperity. It can be applied to everything from fashion to city buildings. True Chinese navigation by compass didn't occur until the eleventh century AD. Chinese scientists didn't explore other uses of magnetism until the first century AD.

The Inventions of Zhang Heng

Zhang Heng (AD 78–139) is credited with helping to devise the grid system used for land maps, among other achievements. An astronomer, mathematician, and geographer, Zhang

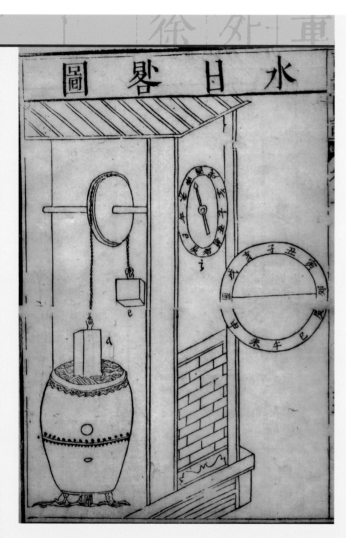

Most scholars credit Zhang Heng as the inventor of the mechanical water clock. The clock pictured above is from 1627, but it worked similar to mechanical water clocks of the first century AD. Water dripped at a constant rate from the hole of a vessel, driving a chain of gears that moved a globe through one revolution each day.

adapted his sky observations to Earth around AD 100. By then, he knew about the equator as well as the north pole and south pole.

This inventive man is also credited with helping to develop the mechanism for the first Chinese mechanical water clock in 124. Zhang is also credited with developing the first seismograph for measuring earthquakes in 132. The device included a bronze vase with a ring. The vase was 8 feet (2.4 m) in diameter and held eight evenly spaced dragon heads near its top. Each dragon head contained a bronze ball in its mouth. Below each dragon head was a toad. Within the vase was a copper shaft containing a pendulum that was connected to each dragon's mouth by a copper arm and that tilted during a tremor, causing the ball to drop from the dragon's mouth to the toad's upturned mouth. The epicenter of the quake was then in the opposite direction of the toad's head.

Counting

Chinese scientists had a great understanding of mathematics, which they described as *suan chu* (the art of calculation). At first, rods called counting sticks were used by placing the sticks

This cutaway of the first seismograph is a reconstruction based on Zhang Heng's bronze invention of AD 132. An earthquake was indicated by the dropping of a ball from a dragon's mouth into the open mouth of a toad. Zhang Heng used a pendulum, which, when tilted by a tremor, pushed a slider device that then pushed a ball out of the dragon's mouth.

into boxes to help determine calculations. Numerical inscriptions that used the decimal place system were found on oracle bones beginning in the fourteenth century BC, showing a high degree of mathematical sophistication.

The Chinese invented symbols for numbers that became the basis of those we use around the world today. By the fourth century BC, they affixed numbers to a tablet known as a counting board. Each board had red rods to indicate positive numbers and black rods to indicate negative numbers. A space was used to acknowledge the number gap caused by moving to two or more digits. For example, the number 101 would be a one followed by a space followed by a one (one hundred, no tens, and one unit). This led to the concept of zero, which aided their calculations. Such counting was later applied to weights, measures, and, eventually,

25

This Chinese abacus, a calculating device, from the nineteenth century AD is the oldest type of abacus still in use. It has thirteen rods that are separated by a crossbar. Using any rod as the unit rod, the rods to the left stand for tens, hundreds, thousands, and so on, while the rods to the right represent tenths, hundredths, thousandths, and so on.

coin money. The Chinese abacus was used as early as the second century BC. It was made of a rectangular frame that held vertical rods. The frame was divided into two decks by a crossbar. Each rod in the upper deck held two beads, with each bead having a value of five. Each rod in the lower deck held five beads, with each bead representing a value of one. When a bead was counted, it was moved to the crossbar. Each vertical rod stood for a place value, such as the 1s, 10s, 100s, and so forth.

CONSTRUCTION, MACHINES, TRANSPORTATION, AND NAVIGATION

The Chinese developed some of the earliest complex machines, allowing them to prosper as farmers, artisans, and merchants, and to tame their land to suit their growing needs. The earliest drilling by the Chinese is believed to have been done in the first century BC. Miners managed to dig about 4,800 feet (1,463 m) deep and used the drill to reach gas deposits.

The control of water also allowed the Chinese to use hydropower for the earliest machines. Water was used to power bamboo devices to help grind grains. Bamboo, a lightweight, sturdy, and plentiful wood, was used to build tools and homes.

The various production techniques, once developed, remained in place for centuries. Change was slow to be adopted.

Chinese builders and carpenters construct a palace during the Shang dynasty (1600–1300 BC). This illustration is from an edition of *Shujing* (The Book of Documents), a compilation of ancient historical records from the Zhou dynasty that dates from around 481 to 221 BC.

Construction and Machines

In home construction, builders added an elaborate set of brackets to support the long projecting eaves that topped the pillars of buildings. These eaves slowly started to turn upward in graceful curves, a distinctive touch still seen in modern Chinese architecture. There are several theories about the reason for these curved eaves. Some historians believe they follow the principles of feng shui, presenting a pleasant skyline. They may have functioned as a barrier to fires. Others believe that the upturned eaves helped to spread the weight of the heavy overhang of the roof. Most building construction during the early dynasties relied on columns to hold up the roof. Screens and curtains served as walls.

In the fourth century BC, the wide-spread use of the double-acting piston bellows greatly improved metalwork. The bellows, which supplied a continuous blast of air when a piston pushed or pulled air into a chamber, didn't exist in Europe for centuries to come. They helped the furnaces burn hotter and longer, which enhanced the ability of blacksmiths to craft tools and weapons. The Chinese adapted the device for pumping fluids, and later used it as a flamethrower.

A mechanism similar to the chain belt was the driving belt, invented in the first century BC. Originally designed to aid in the production of silk, its was soon applied to other areas. The belt enabled energy to be transferred from one wheel to another, providing additional power. Eventually,

This terra-cotta model of a house dates from the Han dynasty in the early 200s BC. The roof of the house features the curved eaves that were an architectural element of the time and that were thought to give structures harmony with certain spiritual forces, as determined by feng shui.

THE GREAT WALL

Nobles built walls to protect their land. Around the second century BC, China's first emperor, Qin Shi Huangdi (formerly Prince Zheng, but he changed his name when he united the city-states), had the various walls throughout the Chinese states joined together. The walls formed the Great Wall of China, which measures between 15 and 30 feet (5–9 m) high; from 15 to 25 feet (5–8 m) thick; and more than 4,000 miles (6,437 km) in length, going from east to west. It took 2,000 years to complete the Great Wall.

The earliest walls were constructed more than 5,500 years ago, using a technique known as *hang-tu*, or "beaten earth." A framework was made from wood or bamboo and then filled with dirt and packed into place using a variety of tools. Each 6- to 8-inch (15- to 20-cm) layer was packed tight before the next was

The Great Wall was built for mostly defense purposes, but its function as a communication backbone through the formidable mountainous terrain was nearly as important. Along the top of the wall, among the battlements and towers, is a road paved with bricks.

added. When the top was reached, the framework was removed and that section of wall was finished. From all studies, *hang-tu* was the only method of construction employed for building the wall over thousands of years. Only a few hundred miles of existing walls made it to the new Great Wall. More than 2,500 miles (4,023 km) of new wall were built at Qin Shi Huangdi's command.

The Chinese laborers loaded woven baskets with dirt, then carried them up ladders and filled in the framework. If stones were to be used, they were pushed up ramps.

The wall was unique in that it had towers, constructed from wood and sun-baked brick and spaced across its length, and a road on the top for traveling. The towers measured 40 feet (12 m) by 30 feet (9 m) at the base, and about 40 feet (12 m) high. Archers fired an arrow twice in a row, using that distance to determine the space between towers and ensuring the army could defend the land with no gap between structures.

the driving belt led to the development of the spinning wheel.

Improving Transportation

The Chinese made improvements in wagons, letting animals pull carts and, eventually, chariots. Under Qin Shi Huangdi's era of standardization, wagon and chariot axles were given a fixed width, which in turn led to the construction of uniform roads.

The Chinese greatly improved sea transportation when they invented the rudder. One of the rudder's earliest representations is in a pottery model of a Chinese ship that was discovered in a tomb from about AD 100. Using a rudder, which was similar to an oar

This bronze guard and chariot with a horse dates from the Han dynasty. Besides inventing the trace harness, which enabled horses to pull heavy loads without injury, the Chinese standardized the axles of chariots, which eventually allowed them to make the measurements of roads uniform.

and could be raised and lowered by rope or chains, helped sailors to gain greater control over directing the course of the boat. Aided by navigational information from the scientists, the Chinese rapidly took to the waters and explored. They were the first visitors to reach Australia, Africa's Cape of Good Hope, and elsewhere in Asia. Some students of Chinese naval history speculate that the Chinese first explored America in 1421, some seventy-one years before Columbus, although this idea is hotly debated.

MEDICINE

The development of medicine in China began with understanding the properties of native plants and life-forms. From there, trial and error enabled people specializing in their use to improve medicines. More than 2,000 years ago, these early pharmacologists worked to perfect an elixir that would extend the lives of the rulers.

In 1999, archaeologists discovered several skulls in a tomb located in the Shandong province. These skulls had triangular holes. This finding suggests that rudimentary surgery, including craniotomy (the surgical opening of the skull), was practiced as early as 4,000 years ago. After many centuries, a growing respect for the body slowed such surgeries in favor of medicinal treatments. Furthermore, given Chinese reverence for the dead, studying cadavers was difficult. Toward the first century BC, the emperors found it agreeable to allow such studies on the bodies of criminals who had been executed by the court.

Rise of the Doctor

Around the sixth century BC, men of medicine were not yet called doctors, but they were treated as a separate class

Shen Nong, who lived during the third millennium BC, is said to have tasted more than 300 herbs to test their medicinal properties. He supposedly wrote the earliest Chinese pharmacopoeia, a book about medicinal preparations and herbs.

of professionals comparable to tribal shamans. Shamans mixed rudimentary folk medicine with spiritual beliefs. Within three centuries, the practice of doctors developed into a separate profession with specialties such as external and internal medicine, and dietary and veterinary science.

Tsou Yen (340–260? BC) was a philosopher who developed the theory of the Five Elements (wood, fire, earth, metal, and water) to explain how the body works. Shen Nong, known as the divine farmer, further refined these into Four Spirits and Five Tastes. The belief of the day was that everything was composed from the five elements. The herbs used as medicines were broken down into the Five Tastes: sweet, salty, bitter, pungent, and sour. How the elements reacted to the tastes was carefully recorded. The human body could respond by becoming cold, hot, warm, or cool. These temperatures represented the Four Spirits.

Tsou Yen felt illnesses were caused by a body's spirit—the two life forces known as yin and yang—being out of balance. The use of needles, known as acupuncture, was one method of healing. Doctors studied the body in great detail to find out which nerves affected which extremities. The needles were thought to restore balance, and thus relieve pain. The use of these needles, first fashioned from stone, dates back nearly 6,000 years or more and is one of the earliest known forms of medicine. The oldest written record about acupuncture appears in the Chinese medical book entitled *The Yellow Emperor's Classic of Internal Medicine*, which is attributed to the legendary Yellow Emperor, Huangdi, of the third millennium BC. Today the book has become a landmark in the history of Chinese civilization.

During the Han dynasty, a variety of herbs had been brought into everyday use, such as ephedra for asthma and seaweed for goiter. By this time, doctors had also determined that peasants subsisting on mainly rice diets were suffering from vitamin deficiencies. The doctors found positive uses for minerals, including iron, copper, and mercury.

Following the other methods of Qin Shi Huangdi's drive for uniformity, doctors all consulted the *Shennong Bencaojing* (Classic of Herbal Medicine), a guide believed to have been written in 100 BC and is the earliest-known book on herbal medicine. Today it is

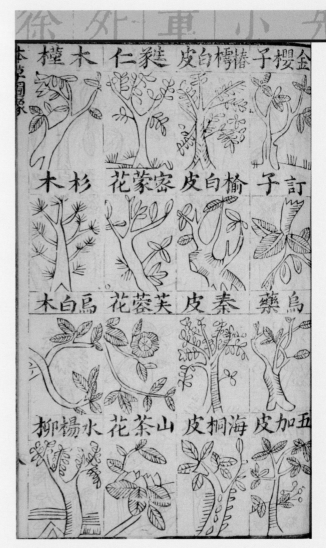

This page from an herbal and medicines book whose author is unknown shows some of the 365 plants that were said to have been studied. The page pictured here is taken from an edition of the book that was published in China in 1740.

not known who wrote the guide, but it was erroneously credited to Shen Nong following the tradition of crediting revered figures of the past with great knowledge.

This painting from the Song dynasty (AD 960–1279) shows a country doctor applying the cure of moxibustion to a man's back. The treatment involves the moxa plant, which is ignited on the skin at acupuncture points to help warm the meridians (the pathways along which the body's vital energy flows according to the theory of acupuncture) and make the blood flow smoothly.

Observations and Improvements

Chunyu Yi (215–167 BC) is considered the first doctor to maintain patient records. Another prominent doctor of the later Han era was Zhang Ji (AD 150–219), who wrote the *Shang Han Za Bing Lun* (Discourse on Fevers and Miscellaneous Illnesses), a book that recommended treatments based on the assessment of symptoms. The first doctor to employ an anesthetic (using *mafeisan*, a powder dissolved in an alcoholic beverage) for a surgical procedure was Hua Tuo (AD 141–208), Zhang Ji's contemporary. Hua was also unique in his insistence on physical exercise for patients.

As with most Chinese developments, Chinese discoveries in medicine either preceded Western cultures or paralleled them. Without these doctors and pharmacologists, the Chinese people would not have prospered.

WARFARE

In the early Zhou dynasty, the leaders recognized that they could not centrally control their vast holdings, so they delegated responsibility to lords, each of whom ruled a walled city. The lord, who inherited his position, was aided by fighting forces, who also inherited their positions. This feudal system remained in place until 770 BC, when several of the vassal states rebelled. As the people and country rapidly flourished, incessant warfare between the different city-states inhibited any sense of political stability.

Men were drafted for two-year tours of duty, generally serving as infantrymen. They served with others from the same province under the command of their local governor or administrator. Professional full-time soldiers remained on duty indefinitely at each state capital.

This sword was manufactured during the Warring States period, around 475 to 221 BC. The sword, made of cast bronze with turquoise inlay, is an example of the advanced casting techniques that were common in China. Bronze was also used for the trigger mechanisms in crossbows, dagger axes, and the clasps or fittings for horse harnesses.

This era, known as the Warring States period (475–221 BC), saw local dukes proclaim themselves king. There were seven competing states or powers—Qi, Yan, Zhao, Wei, Han, Chu, and Qin—fighting one another for the next 300 years.

With all their other inventiveness, the Chinese were quick to learn ways of protecting their people and waging battle. The earliest warriors wore buffalo or rhinoceros hides and carried bows and arrows. The most common weapon used was a knife with a bronze blade. By 400 BC, the two-edged sword was popular, as was the crossbow.

The Crossbow

The crossbow, made from laminated wood, bone, horn, and sinew (which acted as the string) with a metal or bone trigger mechanism, was the weapon of choice for the peasant infantry.

Crossbow arrows proved particularly effective in disabling chariots, forcing a change in the way battles were conducted. Increased use of riders on horseback also improved communications between leaders and armed forces. Also during the fourth century BC, the crossbow was augmented with a magazine containing multiple arrows.

As the casting of bronze was developed, beginning as early as 1800 BC, bronze was first used decoratively. By the Warring States period, the Chinese had refined the casting process to be able to mass-produce bronze weapons. Evidence points to the use of bronze swords during warfare being supplemented with heavy, melon-shaped balls that were either hurled or swung with an attached chain.

During the Shang dynasty, some soldiers wore breastplates of wood or felt. Others were given iron-plate armor (which was sometimes gilded) or flexible armor of chain mail, a concept that had been imported from the Persian west.

The introduction of the stirrup to horse saddles began in the fifth century BC and spread rapidly. This improvement in riding allowed more fighting on horseback with soldiers armed with lances.

The Art of War

Sun Tzu, a general, is credited with having written a book on warfare that is in print to this day. *The Art of War*, written around 345 BC (some historians consider it to be from 498 BC), continues to be studied by military strategists around the world. Historians question whether Sun Tzu wrote the book, but the book's lessons remain valid. For example, he supposedly wrote, "Appear at points which the enemy must hasten to defend; march swiftly to places where you are not expected."

During the Warring States period, battles evolved from skirmishes into

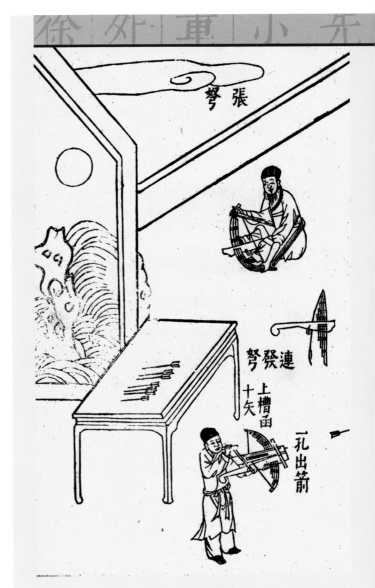

In this illustration from 1637, two men are making and testing crossbows. Invented during the fourth century BC, the crossbow became the common weapon used by Chinese armies because it had greater firing range than the composite bow did.

This terra-cotta archer, who wears a breastplate, was unearthed during the excavation of the tomb of Qin Shi Huangdi in Xian in 1974. The tomb included more than 8,000 life-size men, horses, and chariots.

during this era that bellows were used to pump smoke from burning balls of mustard into tunnels being dug by the enemy. The preferred method of fighting was the cavalry, and it was adopted across the city-states. The use of masses of men as infantry also increased. For example, in 260 BC, in the Battle of Changping between the Qin and Zhao states, the Zhao lost 400,000 men.

Although Qin Shi Huangdi ordered the Great Wall to be built to defend against northern barbarians, he also hired barbarian nomadic tribes from the north to fight for China. These northerners were all raised to forage for their food and were trained to fight on horses with the longbow. As a result, they continued to pose a serious threat to the settlement of China as a great nation.

The inventiveness that allowed the Chinese people to tame and cultivate the land led to centuries of prosperity, punctuated by frequent battles over authority. All along, though, the Chinese prospered and used their newly invented tools, weapons, and technological methods to thrive, laying the foundation for one of the world's longest surviving civilizations.

monthslong sieges against villages. The fighting was described as becoming more violent and victories more decisive, giving rise to the increased power of the military. Even though chemical warfare had been written about hundreds of years before, it was

TIMELINE

Circa 500,000 BC	Earliest humans in the region begin using stone tools.
Circa 7000 BC	Rice is grown.
Circa 6500 BC	Farming communities begin around the Yellow River. Pottery is painted.
Circa 4500 BC	Lacquer, the first plastic, is introduced 3,200 years ahead of Western civilization.
Circa 4000 BC	First evidence of acupuncture being used.
3500 BC	The potter's wheel is invented.
2205 BC	Flood and irrigation controls are introduced.
1800 BC	Bronze begins to be manufactured. The Bronze Age begins.
1400 BC	The decimal place system is introduced in China 2,300 years ahead of the West.
1027 BC	First writing found on bones.
500 BC	Ironwork begins. Row cultivation of crops and intensive hoeing begins 2,200 years before Western invention. The iron plow is used in farming, some 2,000 years sooner than Western invention.
400 BC	Blood circulation is studied 1,800 years before Western civilization. The horse harness is developed 500 years before Western invention.

(continued on following page)

400 BC
(continued)

Double-acting piston bellows, using air and liquid, is invented some 1,900 to 2,100 years before Western invention.

Petroleum and natural gas are used as fuel 2,300 years before Western invention.

The concept of zero is introduced in mathematics.

The first magnetic compass is developed.

Poison gas, smoke bombs, and tear gas are employed by armies.

The crossbow is invented.

217–210 BC

About 1,500 miles (2,414 km) of the Great Wall are constructed.

214–204 BC

The Great Wall is extended and joined to protect the northern border of China.

200 BC

Paper is invented.

The multitube seed drill is invented.

Steel is manufactured from cast iron some 2,000 years before Western civilization.

GLOSSARY

bamboo A woody tropical grass having hollow, woody stems. When dried, these lengthy stems harden and can be used for many purposes.

channel The deeper part of a river, allowing navigable passage.

contour plowing Plowing furrows that follow the curve of the land rather than straight rows; ridges form to slow water flow and preserve topsoil.

eave The overhanging lower edge of a roof that projects into the air.

gelatin A substance formed after boiling skin, bones, or connective tissue from animals.

hemp A fiber from the cannabis plant used to make rope and other items.

lodestone A piece of stone with magnetic properties used to attract metallic objects.

moldboard A curved iron plate that is connected above a plowshare to lift and turn soil.

polestar A star in the constellation of Ursa Minor at the end of the Little Dipper's handle; the northern axis of the earth points toward it.

prophecy A prediction of something to come.

scapulimancy The act of foretelling the future by using tortoise shells and animal shoulder blades.

siege A prolonged blockade of a town to force its surrender.

stirrup The loop at either side of a horse rider's saddle with a flattened bottom to allow the rider's foot to rest in place and used to aid in mounting and riding a horse.

terrace A raised section of soil such as a hillside, with vertical sides and a flat top surface for farming.

vassal A person working and holding land owned by a lord, receiving protection in exchange for allegiance and tithes.

FOR MORE INFORMATION

Asia Society
725 Park Avenue at 70th Street
New York, NY 10021
(212) 288-6400
Web site: http://www.asiasociety.org

Association for Asian Studies
1021 East Huron Street
Ann Arbor, MI 48104
(734) 665-2490
Web site: http://www.aasianst.org

Embassy of People's Republic of China
2300 Connecticut Avenue NW
Washington, DC 20008
Web site: http://www.china-embassy.org/
    eng/default.htm

Freer Gallery of Art/Arthur M. Sackler
    Gallery
Smithsonian Institution
P. O. Box 37012, MRC 707
Washington, DC 20013-7012
(202) 633-4880
Web site: http://www.asia.si.edu

Web Sites

Due to the changing nature of Internet links, the Rosen Publishing Group, Inc., has developed an online list of Web sites related to the subject of this book. This site is updated regularly. Please use this link to access the list:

http://www.rosenlinks.com/taw/teac

FOR FURTHER READING

Cotterell, Arthur. *Eyewitness Guides: Ancient China*. New York, NY: DK Books, 2000.

Debaine-Francfort, Corinne. *Discoveries: Search for Ancient China*. New York, NY: Harry N. Abrams, 1999.

Liu, Chao-Hui Jenny. *Ancient China: 2,000 Years of Mystery and Adventure to Unlock and Discover*. Philadelphia, PA: Running Press Kids, 1996.

McIntosh, Jane. *Civilizations: 10,000 Years of Ancient History*. New York, NY: DK Books, 2001.

Ping, Ming, and Yuan Yang. *The Rise and Fall of the Empires: War Stories in Ancient China*. San Francisco, CA: Foreign Language Press, 2001.

Rawson, Jessica. *Mysteries of Ancient China: New Discoveries from the Early Dynasties*. New York, NY: George Braziller, 1996.

Verstappen, Stefan H. *The Thirty-Six Strategies of Ancient China*. San Francisco, CA: China Books & Periodicals, Inc., 1999.

Woods, Michael, and Mary B. Woods. *Ancient Agriculture: From Forging to Farming* (Ancient Technology). Minneapolis, MN: Lerner Publishing, 2000.

Woods, Michael, and Mary B. Woods. *Ancient Communication: From Grunts to Graffiti* (Ancient Technology). Minneapolis, MN: Lerner Publishing, 2000.

Woods, Michael, and Mary B. Woods. *Ancient Machines: From Wedges to Waterwheels* (Ancient Technology). Minneapolis, MN: Lerner Publishing, 1999.

BIBLIOGRAPHY

BBC News. "China Had First Complex Machines." Retrieved October 28, 2004 (http://news.bbc.co.uk/1/hi/sci/tech/3792819.stm).

Boase, Wendy. *Early China*. New York, NY: Gloucester Press, 1978.

Deady, Kathleen, and Muriel DuBois. *Ancient China*. Mankato, MN: Capstone Press, 2004.

DuTemple, Lesley A. *The Great Wall of China*. Minneapolis, MN: Lerner Publications, 2003.

Ganeri, Anita. *Legacies from Ancient China*. Mankato, MN: Thameside Press, 1999.

Gascoine, Bamber. *The Dynasties and Treasures of China*. New York, NY: Viking Press, 1973.

Li, Dun J. *The Civilization of China*. New York, NY: Charles Scribner's Sons, 1975.

Mitsuru Sôma, Kin-aki Kawabata, and Kiyotaka Tanikawa. "Units of Time in Ancient China and Japan." *Publications of the Astronomical Society of Japan*. Retrieved October 2004 (http://adsabs.harvard.edu/cgi-bin/nph-bib_query?bibcode=2004PASJ...56..887S&db_key=AST&high=426d16b73717424).

Mount, Ellis, and Barbara A. List. *Milestones in Science and Technology: The Ready Reference Guide to Discoveries, Inventions, and Facts*. Phoenix, AZ: Oryx Press, 1987.

Saxakali. "Development of Mathematics in Ancient China." Retrieved October 28, 2004 (http://www.saxakali.com/COLOR_ASP/chinamh1.htm).

Schafer, Edward H. *Ancient China*. New York, NY: Time-Life Books, 1967.

Temple, Robert. *The Genius of China: 3,000 Years of Science, Discovery, and Invention*. New York, NY: Simon and Schuster, 1986.

Walker, Richard L. *Ancient China and Its Influence in Modern Times*. New York, NY: Franklin Watts, Inc., 1969.

Woods, Michael, and Mary B. Woods. *Ancient Warfare: From Clubs to Catapults (Ancient Technology)*. Minneapolis, MN: Runestone Press, 2000.

INDEX

About the Author

Robert Greenberger is the author of nearly a dozen nonfiction books for young adults. A history major from Binghamton University, he has a keen interest in Chinese history and inventions. Mr. Greenberger lives in Connecticut.

Photo Credits

Cover Erich Lessing/Art Resource, NY; cover (inset), p. 25 © Science Museum, London/HIP/The Image Works; p. 4 Bibliotèque Nationale, Paris, France, Lauros/Giraudon/Bridgeman Art Library; p. 6 © A. Karl/ J. Kemp; pp. 10, 26 © SSPL/The Image Works; p. 11 Werner Forman/Art Resource, NY; pp. 12, 17, 24, 39 Max Planck Institute for the History of Science at the Institute for the History of Natural Sciences of the Chinese Academy of Sciences; p. 15 © Royal Ontario Museum/Corbis; p. 16 The Art Archive/British Library; pp. 20, 28 British Library; p. 21 © The British Library/ Topham-HIP/The Image Works; p. 29 Musée Cernuschi, Paris, France, Lauros/Giraudon/ Bridgeman Art Library; p. 30 © Panorama Images/The Image Works; p. 32 © Zhao Guangtian/Panorama/The Image Works; p. 34 Société Asiatique, Collège de France, Paris, France, Archives Charmet/Bridgeman Art Library; p. 35 Courtesy of the National Library of Medicine; p. 36 The Art Archive/ National Palace Museum Taiwan; p.38 Los Angeles County Museum of Art. Gift of Mr. and Mrs. Eric Lidow, photograph © 2005 Museum Associates/LACMA; p. 40 The Art Archive/Dagli Orti.

Designer: Evelyn Horovicz
Photo Researcher: Amy Feinberg